Baby Animals
Giant Coloring and Activity Book

CUTE AND CUDDLY!

Modern Publishing
A Division of Unisystems, Inc.
New York, New York 10022
Printed in the U.S.A.
Series UPC: 47060S2

Zebras

Kittens

Bunny

START

END

LOST LION
This baby lion is trying to make his way back home! See if you can help him by following the correct path through the maze!

SEE ANSWERS

I

Ladybugs

Sea Lion

1

2

3

4

SEE ANSWERS

(2) **SIMILAR SEALS**
Which two seals look exactly the same? Circle your answer!

Panda Bears

Kangaroos

Lobster

SEE ANSWERS

③

HOW MANY BUBBLES?

How many bubbles do you see coming out of the baby fish's mouth? Write your answer on the line!

_____

4

FRIENDLY FOX
How many words can you make using the letters in the words FRIENDLY FOX?

_____   _____

_____   _____

_____   _____

_____   _____

SEE ANSWERS

Hippopotamus

Turtles

Aardvark

1

2

3

4

⑤ **EGG-CELLENT EGGS**
Which nest has the most eggs in it?
Circle your answer.

SEE ANSWERS

Piglets

Ponies

Hamster

6

COOL KOALA
Unscramble the letters to reveal the name of the continent where most Koala Bears are found!

A T R L A S I U A

_ _ _ _ _ _ _ _ _

SEE ANSWERS

Flamingos

Seahorses

7

CHIPMUNK MUNCHIES
Chipmunks like to eat lots of nuts and berries! What do you think this chipmunk is having for dinner today? Draw some ideas in the space below!

Snail

8

FROG WORD SEARCH
Can you find the words about frogs listed below in the puzzle? Look up, down, across and diagonally!

RIBBIT   JUMP   LILYPAD   GREEN

B G R E E N C K
D H I J V B P L
F N B R U K O Y
K A B V G M X C
V F I P R Q P M
L Z T M E S D N
P D A P Y L I L

SEE ANSWERS

9

W IS FOR WOLF

Wolf begins with the letter "W." Can you name 3 other animals that also begin with that letter? Write your answers on the lines!

_____

_____

_____

SEE ANSWERS

Dolphins

Butterflies

COOL CODE
Using the code, write the letters on the line to find out what the cheetah is known for!

1=A   2=B   3=C   4=D   5=E   6=F
7=G   8=H   9=I   10=J   11=K   12=L
13=M   14=N   15=O   16=P   17=Q   18=R
19=S   20=T   21=U   22=V   23=W   24=X
25=Y   26=Z

___ ___ ___ ___ ___ ___ ___
6   1   19   20   5   19   20

___ ___ ___ ___
12   1   14   4

___ ___ ___ ___ ___ ___ !
1   14   9   13   1   12

SEE ANSWERS

Calf

Walruses

11

RHYME TIME
How many words can you think of that rhyme with BEE? See if you can name 5 in under 1 minute! Go!

_____

_____

_____

_____

_____

SEE ANSWERS

PUPPY PATH

Help this puppy get to his dog bowl by following the correct path through the maze!

SEE ANSWERS

Gorilla

Grasshopper

13

MISSING LETTERS

Fill in the missing vowels (A, E, I, O or U) to spell the name of this large animal!

__ L __ PH __ NT

SEE ANSWERS

Eagle

Frogs

Skunks

KITTEN JOKE

Write the letter that comes AFTER each letter given to determine the answer to the joke!

What is a cat's favorite color?

_ _ _ _ _ _ _ _ _

O   T   Q   Q   Q   Q   O   K   D

SEE ANSWERS

Stingray

Giraffes

1

2

3

4

SEE ANSWERS

15

LOOK AT THE LLAMAS
Which baby llama looks different than the others? Circle your answer!

Lamb

16

DOT-TO-DOT
Connect the dots from 1 to 50 to see the baby raccoon!

SEE ANSWERS

17

OSTRICH FRIENDS

An ostrich is a type of bird. Can you name 3 other types of birds? Write your answers on the lines!

_____

_____

_____ SEE ANSWERS

Deer

Polar Bears

1

2

3

4

18

INSECT INSPECTION
Which of the animals is NOT an insect? Circle your answer!

SEE ANSWERS

19

HAPPY HIPPO

A hippo has _____ legs.

A hippo has _____ ears.

A hippo has _____ tail.

SEE ANSWERS

Bumble Bees

Turkeys

Caterpillar

SEE ANSWERS

20

THE WORM WAY
Help this baby chick get to his friend by following the correct path, which is made up of only worms!

Puppies

Snake

AROUND THE WHEEL
To reveal the name of this baby animal, start at the arrow and write down every **THIRD** letter in order on the lines!

21

___ ___ ___ ___ ___ ___ ___

SEE ANSWERS

Sharks

Ostrich

COOL CODE

Using the code, write the letters on the line to find out what a porcupine's body is covered with!

1=A	2=B	3=C	4=D	5=E	6=F
7=G	8=H	9=I	10=J	11=K	12=L
13=M	14=N	15=O	16=P	17=Q	18=R
19=S	20=T	21=U	22=V	23=W	24=X
25=Y	26=Z				

___ ___ ___ ___ ___ ___
17   21   9   12   12   19

SEE ANSWERS

Rhinoceroses

Jellyfish

2 + 3 = ____

3 + 4 = ____

2 + 2 = ____

5 + 1 = ____

MONKEY MATH
Add the number of monkeys together!

SEE ANSWERS

HOW MANY LAMBS?

How many lambs do you see on the page? Write your answer on the line!

_____

SEE ANSWERS

Penguin

SQUIRREL SEARCH

Can you find the words about squirrels listed below in the puzzle? Look up, down, across and diagonally!

SQUIRREL   ACORN   TREE   CLIMB

S A K L U D V
Q B C B V I K
U D F O H J B
I H J K R W M
R X C B V N I
R Z A Q E R L
E E R T F V C
L M L C V K X

SEE ANSWERS

ANSWERS

#1 LOST LION

#2 SIMILAR SEALS

#3 HOW MANY BUBBLES?

8

#4 FRIENDLY FOX

Some possible answers are:

Fry, Rod, Den, Fly, Lend, Lie, Role, For

ANSWERS

#5 EGG-CELLENT EGGS

#6 COOL KOALA

Australia

#8 FROG WORD SEARCH

#9 W IS FOR WOLF

Some possible answers are:

Whale
Walrus
Woodpecker

ANSWERS

#10 COOL CODE

Fastest Land Animal

#11 RHYME TIME

Some possible answers are:

See, Tea, Me, Tree, Knee

#12 PUPPY PATH

#13 MISSING LETTERS

Elephant

ANSWERS

#14 KITTEN JOKE

Purrrrple

#15 LOOK AT THE LLAMAS

#16 DOT-TO-DOT

#17 OSTRICH FRIENDS

Some possible answers are:

Eagle
Robin
Dove
Seagull
Blue Jay

ANSWERS

#18 INSECT INSPECTION

#19 HAPPY HIPPO

A hippo has **4** legs.

A hippo has **2** ears.

A hippo has **1** tail.

#20 THE WORM WAY

#21 AROUND THE WHEEL

Otter

ANSWERS

#22 COOL CODE

Quills

#23 MONKEY MATH

$$2 + 3 = 5$$
$$3 + 4 = 7$$
$$2 + 2 = 4$$
$$5 + 1 = 6$$

#24 HOW MANY LAMBS?

11

#25 SQUIRREL SEARCH

```
S  A  K  L  U  D  V
Q  B  C  B  V  I  K
U  D  F  O  H  J  B
I  H  J  K  R  W  M
R  X  C  B  V  N  I
R  Z  A  Q  E  R  L
E  E  R  T  F  V  C
L  M  L  C  V  K  X
```